3

INDIAN EROTIC STORIES II

JEWEL ALYSSA

Erotic/Romance

Cover image: Pixabay.com

Cover Design: HRK

This is a work of fiction. Names, places, incidents and characters are the product of the author's imagination or used in a fictitious manner. Any resemblance to actual persons, living or dead is entirely coincidental.

No part of this book may be reproduced, distributed or transmitted in any form or by any means including photocopying recording or any other methods without the permission of the author.

Author can be reached by mail.

Jewelalyssa93writer@gmail.com

<u>**WARNING 18+**</u>

This book contains mature content, explicit erotic scenes and language.

Table of contents

<u>Also by Jewel Alyssa</u>

Widow's Desire

The Snake Goddess

The seduced

Sex is serene

The sorcerer 1

The sorcerer 2

The sorcerer 3

Lust is divine

3 erotic stories

The neighbor

The girl next door

My hot neighbor

3 Indian erotic stories

Blue 1: Trapped

Blue 2: Abused

Blue 3: Locked

The neighbor

My name is Rohan. I am twenty. I study in college for B.Com.

My family was very close with our neighbors. Their family has migrated from somewhere in the north and has been living in our neighborhood for last three years.

I was having vacation for summer holidays and was enjoying my time of freedom.

One day the neighbor aunty came to our house for an unusual request.

Her mother in law was admitted in a hospital and her husband was staying back at the hospital. The hospital was far away, somewhere in the northern states.

The daily up and down was not possible. She and her kids were alone at home and they needed someone to be with them.

She requested my mom to send me with them to stay at night at their house.

My mom couldn't deny her request.

She called me and said. "Rohan, you are having a vacation. So you should stay at her house at night. Uncle is far away and they are feeling unprotected. It is our duty to keep them feels secure."

I didn't have a choice.

Let me introduce the aunty now.

Her name is Subha. She is thirty three. She is around 5 foot 3. Her skin was a little tanned, black hair and had a plump body. She had big breasts and back.

I would admit I have jerked off thinking about her a lot of times.

She was an amazing lady, sexy to be honest. Even the sight of her would make my cock hard.

She has two kids, both girls. One is 8 and the other is 5. Maybe because of that she liked me.

I had freedom in that house. She used to call me if she needed to buy groceries and other stuff, even sanitary napkins for her.

Subha looked at me and smiled. "Have dinner with us tonight." she invited.

I looked at my mom. She neither supported nor opposed leaving me confused. I waited for a few more minutes for her to say something but she doesn't even notice me.

Mom and Subha started talking about her mother in law and her illness. I decided to leave them alone.

At 7 in the evening my mom called me and said.

"It is better if you go there before dark."

"Ok mom."

"Have your supper there. She may have made something for you. Don't be greedy and eat slowly." She smirked.

I changed into my night dress, a loose pajamas and vest. I was wearing nothing under the pajamas. I am sure I would be sleeping in the hall.

Their house had only two bedrooms. In one of them Subha and her husband would be sleeping and the other would be the kids bedroom.

I reached their home gleefully. I was happy that I would be able to stare at her, watch her for hours with my stealthy eyes.

The kids were also happy to see me. We played card games and board games. How the time went, we never knew. At 9, Subha called us for dinner.

She served dinner and while serving her big tits wriggled against my back. Though it happened unknowingly my prick was hard in a moment.

After dinner the children went to sleep in their room and I sat at the hall watching TV.

The hall room had four chairs but no couch. I thought I would have to sleep on the floor. *Fuck that.*

Subha finished her dinner and came to the hall and asked me. "Are you sleepy?"

"Yes aunty." I said.

"Come with me." she instructed and walked away. I followed her and we reached their bedroom.

"We don't have an extra bedroom. So you can sleep here."

"Give me a bed sheet and a pillow." I said.

"Why a bed sheet and pillow?" she was surprised.

"I will sleep on the floor." I replied.

She shook her head. "Sleeping on the cold floor will give you back ache in the morning. Sleep with me in the bed." her voice was solid but tempting.

My heart was filled with joy.

I dreamt of touching her in the sleep, caressing her big melons and feeling the heat of her thick cunt.

My rod was getting hard and tried to hide it with my hands.

I quickly lay on my stomach so that she won't see my cock aroused.

I heard the bathroom door getting closed.

After a few seconds she came back wearing a smooth silky night gown.

I saw her hard nipples. Uff, my rod was erect again. At that moment I knew my rod will be hard all night.

She switched the lights off and lay beside me. Few moments later I knew she was asleep.

I slide closer to her so there was hardly a little gap remained between us. She was on her back. I lay sideways facing towards her, my hard cock too close to her hips.

It was a full moon night and the moonlight came through the window. I could see her chest rising with each breath she took.

I wanted to grab them, bite those nipples and nibble all over her big breasts all night.

She twitched in her sleep towards me. Her tits pressed against my chest, her thighs touching my throbbing cock and her hand around me. My cock was vibrating on her thighs and I couldn't move back.

She wasn't wearing any bra inside. Her breasts were loose and squeezed against me. My heart was thumping inside.

Now I could feel her hand sliding down from my back and grabbing my cock.

I gasped for a moment. It was the first time someone holding my cock.

Suddenly she jumped up and switched on the table lamp. She saw me; my eyes open wide and staring at her.

"I...I" she stuttered. "I thought it was my husband. I am sorry." She apologized.

I was also voiceless but I managed to reply her. "It's ok. I also thought so."

My voice made her relax. "Do you have a girlfriend?"

Shyly I replied, no.

She leaned onto the bed again closer to me. I can feel her warm breath hitting on my face. She was horny, I knew.

I kept my hand on her shoulder. She didn't resist. I moved closer and let my cock touch her thighs. Again she seemed unperturbed.

I slid my hand and kept on her melon and nibbled her nipple with my thumb.

A soft moan escaped her mouth. That was encouraging.

"Can I?" she asked. But before she completed my cock was inside her fist. She held it forcibly, feeling the hardness of my rod. As her pressure increased I gripped her melon hard.

We both groaned at the same time.

I kissed her and she opened her mouth to let my tongue enter. I let her suck my tongue.

Now I was over her, my both hands squeezing each of her breasts.

She pushed me and asked me to undress. While I did she removed her maxi revealing her plump body.

I saw her thick cunt lips, big breasts, hard aroused nipples and curvy belly.

I was all heated up now. My cock was really hard even ready to pierce through any metal.

I sucked her nipples and nibbled around her tits with my tongue. I kissed her all over her body.

We were on bed again when I tongued her belly button. She writhed with pleasure.

She pushed me down till my head was between her legs; my tongue was over her clit.

I can smell her pussy, a mesmerizing odor coming from her cunt slowly blinding my senses.

This was my first time of having a chance to smell a cunt.

I badly wanted to feel the insides of a cunt and I inserted my finger inside her.

It was heavenly soft and wet. I pushed my finger in and out smoothly. I added another one.

Sweet moans came out of Subha's mouth. She opened her legs wide for me.

I took out my wet fingers. They were covered with translucent white fluid. The aroma was all around me now. I was being hypnotized by the fragrance of her cunt juice.

I started licking her wet cunt and felt her cunt honey on my tongue. It felt ecstatic.

She lifted her ass for me and my tongue trailed down to her butt hole.

After a while, she pushed me down to the bed and started stroking my cock.

"This is good. This is better than my husband." She whispered.

She took my hard muscle in her mouth till its end touch her throat. She stroked it with her mouth and it felt like heaven.

She climbed on top of me and rubbed her moist cunt on my cock. Then she slid it inside her pussy and started pushing it in and out gently.

It went inside her smoothly as her cunt was leaking lots of honey.

We both gasped and moaned at the same time.

Her hips movements became fast and the sound of her butt cheeks hitting my groin filled the room.

I squashed her tits with my hands and nibbled with my fingers.

Then she asked me to be on top and do the work. We changed positions. I was on top now.

She guided my cock into her cunt. I forced my wood hardly into her pussy. I felt my cock rubbing her cunt walls. She was all wet and heated up. Her cunt honey was drooling out.

She held my butt cheeks and controlled my speed of action.

I wasn't stopping; my cock entered her cunt and exited in rhythm with full force hitting her womb with a pleasurable tempo.

She moaned and groaned uncontrollably.

Her voices filled the room and it made me more enthusiastic. I hit her womb hard with all my strength.

I filled her cunt with my cream. I thrusted again and again till the last drop of my cream was inside her.

I lay on top of her squeezing her tits under my chest with my cock still inside her cunt.

She kissed me with passion.

Her hands squashed my butt and she inserted one finger in my ass hole. She moved her finger in and out which gave me an unimaginable pleasure.

She was still moaning and she inserted one more finger into my butthole. Two fingers were too tight. I felt a little pain but I didn't mind. I let her do whatever she would like to do.

She pushed my ass gently so my soft cock still moves inside her cunt.

"Can you fuck me again?" she asked. "I want more."

"My cock is now soft." I said. "Let me clean it. And you can suck it and make it hard."

"There is no need of cleaning. Just give it in my mouth."

"But it is covered with my creamy milk."

"I will happily taste and swallow it."

I removed my cock from her cunt. As it was out I saw loads of cum running down her pussy.

I took the cum in my hands and poured it into her mouth.

"Have my cum."
She swallowed happily.

I, then put my cum covered cock into her mouth. She sucked and licked the cum. I fucked inside her mouth to make it hard.

Soon we were ready for a second round.

*****_____*****

******_______******

Sexual fever

My name is Anand. This is a story about my first experience. I want to share with you that how your boring fever days could also be exciting.

I was studying in technical college.

My house was in the centre of a huge plot. Our neighbours were Ayyappan and his wife, Swati and their three children.

Their eldest girl is Arya, 26 years of age. Marriage proposals were coming for her but there was a fault in her stars. Her link with Mars is at imperfection.

I never understood these things.

They said she should only get married to a person with same star defects.

Swati Aunty was so beautiful and her children got her features.

Our families were close. We used to play together from our young ages.

Arya mostly used to be at our home. She was so helpful to my mother. She always helped her in kitchen chores.

Even I and my sister thought our mother always gave preference to Arya than us.

It was my vacation period.

One day I became ill. I went to the doctor and got the prescriptions. Doctor advised me to take rest for a few days.

That was a Saturday. The next day we had a marriage to attend.

Fever was low but I felt dizziness and body pain. So I decided to stay back.

Everyone else left with food prepared and set on the table for me.

I slept for a little while.

That time Arya came in.

I was still under the blanket. She checked my forehead. "There is no fever now. Why didn't you go to attend the marriage?"

"I still feel dizzy. And I am feeling cold."

She sat beside me and checked her cell phone. She was doing something, browsing and checking facebook or whatsapp when I was shivering.

She saw me and asked. "What happened, Anand?"

She could see me shivering.

She lay beside me and I adjusted a little to give her space. She lifted the blanket a bit and came inside.

I was on my back and she was on her side facing me.

I didn't felt anything that time.

She kept her hand on my naked chest.

I was wearing only a cotton *lungi* wrapped around my waist. I wasn't wearing a shirt.

She laid closer to me. Her big breasts were brushing my arms.

I felt an electric vibration passing through my body for a split second.

My rod was arousing.

She moved closer. She wrapped her hand around me. Her head was so close to mine and I can feel her hot breaths on my cheek. Both her tits were over my arms and chest as half her body was leaning over me.

"My heat will help you relax. You won't shiver now." I noticed the change in her tone. She was having a mood change.

My rod was in its full form now. It stood straight pointing skywards lifting my *lungi* and the blanket. I wasn't wearing any briefs.

Unexpectedly, Arya kept her one leg over mine, her lower part of the thigh too close to my erect pole.

I felt my cock quivering.

"Don't you feel comfortable now?" she asked. She wasn't calm but regularly moved, as her breasts rubbed me and her body brushed me.

Her knee touched my pole for an instant.

I hummed in a positive way.

My heart was beating fast. She must have noticed that as her hand was on my chest.

"I will hug you tightly so you will feel more warmth." She said.

She tilted her body again as her hug tightened. Her knee was touching my rod.

Yes, she noticed that. She lifted her head and looked down.

I am sure she saw the tent created by my cock.

I have a nine inch cock which made a really noticeable tent between my legs. She was not going to miss that.

I knew her hand going down from my chest. I knew my cloth sliding away from my cock. Her leg was off from my leg. After some time it was back again on my chest and her leg slid over my *lungi* sliding it sideways. Her thighs ride over my cock pressing it to my body. Her thigh was naked as was my cock.

She slid the cloth away from my cock and pulled up her skirt till her waist.

I can feel her wet cunt brushing against my hip.

She gave a little peck on my cheek and asked whether I am better now.

I replied yes and asked her how she was feeling.

"I need more than a hug to feel well." She replied.

She rubbed my cock with her thigh.

I turned towards her and hugged her. My lips met hers. My chest was against her breasts. My cock was between her thighs.

I nibbled her lips as she sucked them. Her breasts were getting squeezed against my chest.

"Oh Anand." She moaned.

She was feeling desperate. She was ready for anything and everything.

She wanted my cock and I wanted her cunt.

I can feel her heat, her thirst, and her lusty desires. I wasn't going to deny her the pleasure she was craving for.

I sucked her upper lips and she did my lower lips. I removed the blanket from our top.

My *lungi* was open and my ass open. My cock was between her thighs as she pressed it with her inner thighs.

I saw her naked part of the ass as her skirt was raised maximum.

My hand ran over her ass and inserted my finger into her ass hole.

She was in ecstasy.

Our lubricants leaked and made us wet.

I made her lie on her back and freed my rod. She opened her legs and I saw her swollen cunt. I was seeing a cunt for the first time.

"Lick my cunt." She moaned.

Small shards of hair raised above her clit as she must have shaved days back.

Her cunt looked like a lotus flower.

I took my face close to her pussy.

I smelled the sweet aroma of her flower. I kissed her cunt lips.

She lifted her hips in excitement. I heard her soft gasps. I saw her squeezing her breasts. She licked her lower lips.

She was so aroused with lust.

I started to lick her clit. With my each lick her body was twitching. I felt her small vibrations at her hips.

My tongue trailed over her cunt lips making her twitch even more. She was wet. She was melting like ice. I was on fire.

I opened her lips and licked her pussy. She was getting wetter. Her cunt was dripping honey.

She hummed, moaned and groaned with pleasure.

I bit her clit softly. She lifted her hips with ecstasy.

I licked the entrance of heaven.

Well, I am not a poet but I did write a poem with my tongue in her cunt for around twenty minutes.

She was moaning continuously.

"I am coming." She said.

She pressed my head between her thighs. I nibbled her cunt lips as her honey came in my mouth.

I drank it whole not letting even a drop go out.

It was now her turn. She pulled me towards her and pushed me onto the bed.

She kissed my lips and her lips trailed down to my chest. She looked at my 9 inch hard pole with excitement.

She held it in her fist and started stroking. I saw her eyes beaming with disbelief.

She used both her hands to stroke it. She was enjoying having my rod in her hands. "I didn't know you had such a big cock." She looked at me.

She kissed the pole head and tongued around it. She opened her lips to give entry into her mouth. Then she took it deep into her throat.

"Oh fuck." I never felt such a delight before. All my veins were getting tight and suddenly it happened.

Warm cream jumped out of my rod and it was in her mouth.

She took in her mouth and showed the cream on her tongue. I watched as she swallowed my cum.

She didn't let it soften as her hands stroked my cock with all her strength.

She sat on my top in such a way the my cock rested on me between her pussy lips.

She rocked her hips as her cunt lips rubbed on my cock making it rock hard again.

She wanted it now.

She rocked over my cock head as it went inside. She leaned over me and pushed her body back to help the rod get inside her pink flower.

She pushed again and again lifting her ass as almost half the length of my rod was inside her cunt.

She was finding it difficult to ride on my rod because of its length. It was tight too.

She asked me to do for her instead. She freed the stiff pole from her cunt and lay on the bed with her legs wide apart.

I leaned over her pushing my rod inside her. She helped the pole head inside her pussy.

She gasped with pain.

"Go in softly." She said.

I pushed my body and pulled back with gentle strokes as the rod rocked and rolled inside her.

My rod was only going in half the length so the next time I rammed into her with full force.

She screamed aloud as the cock went three quarters inside with great intensity.

She squirmed with pain and pleasure as I rammed inside her continuously.

Her soft moans turned into high pitch groans and yet she encouraged me to hit hard.

She was nearing her orgasm as I was almost at my climax.

My cock has swollen inside her and her honey seeped and gave a smooth friction to my movements.

I used all my might as I felt my climax almost certain.

We both came together almost at the same time. My cream filled her entire cunt. When I removed my cock the cream poured out with her honey.

We both looked at it with satisfaction.

We were breathing heavily.

"Let's sleep now. When we wake up, you will be perfectly alright." She said, breathing frantically.

I kissed her lips one more time and nibbled her nipples.

We lay together in the bed naked.

Sleep slowly took care of our tired bodies.

*****_____*****

******________******

Virgin predator

I stood naked in front of the mirror, checking my curves.

What made him love me? Or is it just lust? I wonder.

My breasts were still firm. They aren't too big but still had the shape and size to lure anyone.

No one would call me chubby; I am a medium sized lady.

My body hasn't lost its shape, just a little fat here and there.

I looked at my swollen cunt. My cunt lips were open. My clitoris stood aroused.

A smile twitched between my lips.

What should I do? Shall I go with him or not? That was my confusion. My mind said me to control my carnal urges but my body wasn't ready to listen.

What if anyone sees us together? Everyone will blame me. They will call me a bitch and a whore.

I am fifty one now. I am too old to be active in sex according to the society. Who are they to decide what a woman needs and stop her from having fun?

I was been single for almost seventeen years when my husband ran away with a girl never to come back. I was pregnant at that time and he needed a cunt badly.

In the shock, I lost my child and never had any physical pleasures until him…

I thought about him, his long hair, bright eyes and playful attitude and the care he gave me.

I am his teacher and he is my student. He is only twenty. He is young, energetic and explosively active.

What if anyone knew?

I was feeling worried.

As his teacher, I should not entertain this, my mind warned me.

But my body wanted more, can see my nipples harden and feel my cunt getting wet at the thought of him.

My sexual desires were rising. I wish he was here now.

The memories came to me, as clear as water.

Mahesh wasn't the brightest of students but was active in other curricular activities.

He wasn't a champion but he was good.

I liked him as a student though he was outspoken.

It was one day after the classes of the last day at college, I saw him sitting in the class alone.

I was ready to go home. I went in.

"Why are you here? Why are you not going home?" I asked.

The one week study leave was starting from tomorrow for the final exams.

"I knew you weren't left and you will come here." He stood up from his seat and walked towards me.

My purse was on the table.

"You should go home now and start preparing for the exams. It is way past college hours." I said.

He didn't reply. But I noticed he was looking at my body. His eyes were greedy. I felt disturbed. Or was his stare arousing something long hidden in me?

"Why are you staring at me like this?" I asked.

"You shouldn't come to college wearing sleeveless clothes."

His stare was at my chest.

"What is wrong with sleeveless dress? I am above fifty and no one would mind me wearing anything."

"That's what you think but for me you look like thirty five. I always lose control when I see your shaven, sweating underarms."

I was flattered to be honest.

"You look amazing and your sex appeal is glowing high."

"So you like only my underarms?" I asked. I can feel an unknown wave in my body. I liked the way he is speaking now.

He was standing right in front of me.

"I can see only underarms now. If I see other parts then I will say what all I like." He replied. Suddenly he lifted my hand and kissed under the arm.

I was stunned.

My body twitched for an instant.

I took a step back.

He took another step forward and again kissed and licked my underarms.

I was melting. His hot breaths hit my flesh.

It was a feeling I long thrived for but not now. No, I cannot encourage this. He is only a student.

"What are you doing?" I pushed him away. But he wanted more.

I was in his hold. Unknowingly I lifted my arm and his face dug under it. He licked and kissed continuously.

First time in all these years I was feeling a man. I was not me anymore. I felt the beads on my chest stiffening and a strange throb ripening between my legs. A mysterious sensation long forgotten filled my body.

Something was touching my thighs. I knew what it is. It was patting against me inviting to be freed. He pressed it against my legs.

I gasped. My breath was irregular now.

He freed me and unzipped his trousers. He released his prisoner and I couldn't take my eyes off it.

How many years have passed since I have seen a cock?

It wasn't huge but definitely strong and attractive. It twitched in its position tempting me.

"Uff." A gasp of hot air escaped from my already heated up body.

He took my hand and made me hold his cock. It shook in my fist hardening even more. I hold it tight as wanted it in my fist for a long time.

"Did you like it?" his stare directed into my eyes.

"Yes." I was honest.

"Can we stay here longer?" he asked, kissing on my lips.

"Yes." I felt my panties moist with my cunt honey.

He grabbed my boobs and started pressing them. Ohh, I wanted that badly.

I was waiting for this moment.

He crushed my tits with wild excitement as I stroked his cock with same passion.

He removed my top.

"Here?" I asked.

He threw it to the table.

"Yes teacher."

"Call me Leela." I demanded as he was crushing my boobs over my pink lace bra.

He walked me to the front row of the class room as he threw his clothes somewhere. He climbed on top of a desk and stood naked in front of me. His cock twitched at me.

Then he climbed down to chair. I walked towards him.

I grabbed his throbbing pole.

"In your mouth, Leela." He said.

I was reluctant at first. I haven't had a cock in my mouth for a long time. Even my husband gave his cock only a few times.

"What happened? You never had it in your mouth?"

I couldn't say I forgot to suck dick.

"Open your mouth." He said.

I obeyed my predator.

Yes, I wanted to be his prey. My body was in full submission.

I walked closer to him and opened my mouth. He entered in my mouth and he held my head.

It rested on my tongue for a moment and then quivered.

I wanted to take back my head but his hold was tight.

"Suck it now. You will enjoy, I promise."

I sucked as he said. I was starting to like what I was doing. His cock throbbed in my mouth.

As I licked and sucked his pole was getting harder and I was getting addicted.

Is his cock a drug? I know it is. A highly addictive drug!

He pushed himself with the rhythm of my mouth.

He was trying to get it as deep as he can.

Then he climbed down and removed my bra. I don't know which corner he threw that too. We both didn't care.

He nibbled my exposed tits and its stiff beads.

My cunt was throbbing.

He bit my nipples hard which made me shriek.

"I love you Leela. I was crazy for you."

I didn't know what to say. Part of me said this is wrong. He is my student. He is too young. But the other part of me said to get fucked by him. My pussy wanted a cock badly. After such long years my cunt is wet now. How can I deny my thirst? I never knew I wanted this so desperately. I was itching for this.

He was nibbling on my beads. I smile at the thought that he likes my boobs very much.

With one hand he pulled my black leggings down and I helped him do that.

He threw the cloth to some pat. He wasn't even looking. His face was dug into my tits. His tongue was trailing all over my tits, licking and sucking my nipples.

I squealed as he bit my nipples. He loved doing that. I liked it too since He wasn't biting hard to hurt me. It was soft yet giving a sweet pain.

We were standing in the centre of the classroom. I was having only panties on my body. He was now completely naked.

His young throbbing cock was in my hands. I felt like I want it in my mouth.

I kneeled and took it in my mouth. He was happy when I did that.

I sucked his cock well. I licked his balls and took them in my mouth. He was feeling pleasure as he moaned and twitched his hips.

"Leela, I want to fuck you now." he said. It was like he was my husband or boyfriend. He had that authority in his voice.

I stood up looking into his eyes. He kissed my lips.

He slowly pulled my green panties down. "Aah." He produced a sound of excitement. I looked down. My panties were wet and I saw my slimy white honey sticking to my panties. He was excited to see that!

He took the panties closer to his face and smelled it.

I was wondering what he was doing. Then I realized this was his time. That was why he was so fired up.

"This smell is indescribable. I never knew a cunt has such an incredible aroma."

I was flattered when He said that.

He licked my panties once to savor my honey. I didn't know what my honey tastes like. I was ashamed to ask him.

Then he licked all of it from my panties like he went crazy. Then he quickly came between my legs and started licking my cunt.

"Uff."

I can't say how I was feeling. The sensation made me quiver for a moment like an electric shock.

My cunt lips were open. My clit was raised high. His tongue sucked all the honey from my dripping cunt.

Then he bit my clit hard.

"Oh fuck." I screamed.

He jumped up and covered my mouth.

"Lower your voice." He whispered in my ears.

"That hurt." I said.

"Sorry, I was excited." He apologized.

He made me turned around. His hands brushed my ass and went between his cheeks. He inserted a finger in ass.

I was wondering what all things he is doing. My husband only watched my ass. He never bothered to touch it. This boy is inserting a finger in my asshole. Definitely he has gone crazy. He inserted one more finger and slowly pushed in and out.

I was allowing him to do whatever he wants to. I have completely surrendered to him. He was teaching me new ways of excitement and pleasure.

I bent myself a little for him to play well in my ass. He was standing at my side and I cupped his balls. His one hand was on my breast and other in my ass. His fingers were quickly going in and out.

I tried to moan as softly as I can.

He took out his fingers from my ass and slapped my ass cheeks.

Then he put them in my cunt. I was wondering when he was going to fuck me.

I couldn't wait to have his cock inside my pussy. I want a ride badly.

"I am mad for your ass, Leela. I love you. You belong to me now and forever."

"I am yours Mahesh." I replied. What made me say that, I don't know? I was mad with lust.

While I said he rammed his cock inside my cunt.

"Uff." I gasped.

After a long time I was having a cock inside my cunt. It was almost dry for seventeen years and now Mahesh has made it flourish with honey. How can I not love him?

He rammed into me again and again. I was squirming with the force.

"Slowly Mahesh." I said.

But he wasn't listening. Instead he was pushing harder.

"I love your cunt Leela. I want to fuck you again and again."

I was dripping honey again and he was fucking me easily now.

"Leela I am coming." He shrieked. "I want to come in you."

I wanted to say no. but before that I felt his cream in me and his thrusts slowing down.

He took out his cock from my cunt.

Loads of cream and honey fell down to the classroom floor from my cunt.

We both were panting heavily. I looked at him with gratitude and satisfaction.

"I want it every day. Will you give me Leela?" He asked. "You are my first."

He is a virgin. I was surprised. He did like he was experienced. My virgin predator.

I didn't reply. Instead I hugged him pressing my boobs onto his chest.

It was getting late.

"Come tomorrow Leela." He said. I was picking up my clothes from different parts of the classroom. He took my panties and said. "I want this. I want to smell it all night."

I had to agree. I kissed his cock. I was the first to claim its virginity.

We went home. The whole week we met at this classroom and had sex.

The next two weeks were exams and we couldn't even enter the college premises.

On the last day he had an unusual request.

He wanted to go to Goa with me for a one week tour.

He wants to fuck me all day and night to cope with the loss of two weeks.

I accepted in an instant. But now…

I looked at the mirror again. Tomorrow is the day. He will come in the morning to pick me. I am sure he will fuck me before we leave.

My body tickled at the thought. My wet became wet.

I am desperately counting minutes. I want this night to end fast.

Mahesh, your Leela is waiting with legs wide open for my boy.

*****_____*****

******_______******

www.ingramcontent.com/pod-product-compliance
Lightning Source LLC
Chambersburg PA
CBHW061726130726
47996CB00006B/2524